UN-FAIR

THE SECRET KNOCK CLUB

THE SPRING UN-FAIR

BY **Louise Bonnett-Rampersaud**

PICTURES BY **Adam McHeffey**

two lions

two lions

Text copyright © 2012 by Louise Bonnett-Rampersaud

Illustrations copyright © by Amazon Content Services LLC

Published by Two Lions, New York
www.apub.com

Amazon, the Amazon logo, and Two Lions are trademarks of
Amazon.com, Inc., or its affiliates

Library of Congress Cataloging-in-Publication Data available upon request.
ISBN 9780761463269 (Paperback)
9780761462163 (eBook)

Book design by Anahid Hamparian
Editor: Margery Cuyler

To the original Agnes Mary Murphy (O'Toole)
1917-2009
Rathvilly, County Carlow, Ireland

Contents

Chapter 1

I TAPPED FUDGY ON THE SHOULDER.

"Read it and give it to Heather," I whispered.

You pass notes in class when you want to be polite and not disturb the teacher.

Fudgy read the note and handed it to Heather.

The Heather that is my new, old friend.

This is what that means: It means we *were* friends.

And then we *weren't* friends.

And now we're friends again.

It's a lot to keep track of.

I write it all down on my calendar. If we're friends, I put a check on the day. If we're not, I put an X.

Last year was pretty much an X year.

Only then I found out something good about Heather when we did a community service dog show at the Brookside Retirement Village.

I found out Heather was a jealous person.

Jealous of *me* over a boy!

A boy named Alex-not-Andrew.

Alex-not-Andrew is a twin.

He's Alex.

Not Andrew.

So that's what he calls himself: Alex-not-Andrew.

Heather was jealous that he might like me better. She said I was more "like-ier" than her.

Once I found out that news, we became friends again.

Jealousy can be good for friendships.

That's why she's now in The Secret Knock Club. There're six of us in the club. Me, Fudgy, Heather, Emma, Skipper, and The Cape.

We each use a secret knock to get into our clubhouse.

That's why we're the Secret *Knock* Club.

And that's why I was passing Heather a note.

To give her some Top Secret club information.

Only then Mrs. Carrick started passing out some of her own papers.

Mrs. Carrick is not our real-alive teacher.

She's a substitute.

You call substitutes "subs" for short.

But not the sandwich kind.

One kind of sub

Mrs. Duncan, our real-alive teacher, was visiting her mother, who was sick. We weren't exactly sure when she would be back.

Another kind of sub

"Take one and pass it to the person behind you," Mrs. Carrick said, handing a stack of papers to the first person in each row. "This will help you practice your *g*'s," she said. "Trace the first letter

11

and then try some on your own."

Third grade is when you learn cursive.

Only here's something I found out about that: It's not the swearing kind.

It's the writing kind.

I call it roller-coaster writing because all the letters have loops and curves.

And sometimes you feel kind of sick when you're finished.

Fudgy took the papers and passed them back to me.

Mrs. Carrick turned to check the agenda book. The back of her head looked just like a soft-serve ice-cream cone. A vanilla and chocolate swirled one.

Suddenly, I wanted lunch.

"Read it," I mouthed to Heather, while Mrs. Carrick's head was turned.

Heather opened the note. She put it in her lap, just in case Mrs. Carrick's ice-cream head had eyes in the back of it.

Adults have those a lot.

Mrs. Carrick reached in her purse for her glasses. She put them on the front-of-her-head eyes.

Our real-alive teacher, Mrs. Duncan, has glasses that hang from her neck on a string.

They look like they're bungee jumping.

Mrs. Carrick's don't jump.

They're not the adventurous kind.

"It looks like you'll have a test on writing the first half of the alphabet in cursive on Monday," she said, flipping through the pages of the book. "So keep practicing," she said, facing the class again.

Only here's the thing. Heather was still looking down when Mrs. Carrick started passing out more papers. Mrs. Carrick walked over to Heather's desk.

Heather didn't look up.

Mrs. Carrick peeked over Heather's desk.

She stared at Heather's lap.

"I see you already have your own paper,

honey," she said. She took it out of Heather's hands. "Is this something you would like to share with the class?"

There is a word for when a teacher catches you passing notes in class.

BUSTED.

Chapter 2

HEATHER, FUDGY, AND I STOOD IN FRONT OF Mrs. Carrick's desk.

Fudgy admitted to passing the note so he could stay in during recess to be close to the candy jar.

Fudgy never misses a chance to be close to candy.

All the other kids were outside.

I started to explain.

"Mrs. Carrot," I said.

"It's Car*rick*," she interrupted, before I could get any further.

I was not off to a good start.

But then I saw the lunch Mrs. Carrick had brought sitting on her desk. It was full of green and vegetable things. She was a health nut like my mom! We had something in common. Now I was sure I could fix things.

"I can always tell when people are nuts," I said proudly. "My mom is, too, so I have a lot of experience with nuts." I winked at Mrs. Carrick to let her know I understood her.

She did not wink back.

I looked out the window.

I wanted to be outside enjoying recess like everyone else.

Emma and Skipper were arguing with Colin Holt over who was out in Four Square.

The Cape had just been hit in the head with a basketball.

And a bunch of other kids were chasing each other with worms when the playground lady wasn't looking.

Mrs. Carrick swallowed her green and vegetable things.

"Now about this . . ." she started, holding

up the Top Secret note. "Anyone care to explain?"

Fudgy was still busy staring at the candy jar on the desk.

Heather was busy looking down at the floor, which is what she always does when she gets in trouble.

So it was up to me.

"That's easy," I said. "Don't you know about the fire, throw-up, flood, or blood rule?"

"I'm afraid not" Mrs. Carrick said, shaking her head. "But something tells me I'm about to."

"Well, Mrs. Duncan, our real-alive teacher, has a rule that we can only interrupt her while she's talking if it's about a fire, throw-up, flood,

CLASS RULE #37
DON'T INTERRUPT TEACHER UNLESS THERE'S...
• FIRE
• THROW-UP
• FLOOD
—OR—
• BLOOD

or blood. And this wasn't, so I didn't want to interrupt class."

Fudgy reached for the candy jar.

"Not now," Mrs. Carrick said, swatting her hand at Fudgy like he was a fly or something.

She shook her head again, as if it were coming loose. "So you passed a note instead?"

"Yes," I said, in my always-thinking-of-others voice.

She opened the note. "Well, let's see what was so important it couldn't wait until the end of class."

She read the note. "What's unfair?" she asked, glaring up at us. She looked confused. Like maybe she wished there *had* been a fire, throw-up, flood, or blood.

"The Spring Fair," I said.

"The Spring Fair?"

"Yep," I replied. "No dunk tank."

"No dunk tank?"

"No dunk tank," I said, shaking my head. She still had confused eyes. "I can explain," I continued.

"Please do," she said, nodding.

"Every year we have a Spring Fair at school. You know. Moon bounces. Cake walks. Book sales. The works. And every year the very best thing about the fair is the dunk tank."

18

I turned to Heather and Fudgy.

"Right guys?" I said.

"Right!" they said, nodding.

Although I could tell Fudgy was thinking that maybe it was the cake walk.

"But guess what?" I said, looking back at Mrs. Carrick.

"Go on, " she said, lifting one of her eyebrows up high, like it was trying to crawl off her head.

"This year the school doesn't have enough money to rent the dunk tank. That's what!

19

It's going to be the worst fair EVER. That's why we're renaming it the Spring *Un*-Fair." I tapped the note. "Just like it says right there."

Mrs. Carrick nodded. And then she took off her not adventurous glasses. "Even though you shouldn't pass notes in class, I think I know why this is so important. I'm going to have to agree with you on this one, kids. A Spring Fair without a dunk tank does sound like a Spring *Un*-Fair," she said. "But guess what?"

"What?"

"Aren't you part of The Secret Knock Club I've heard so much about?"

We nodded.

"And didn't I hear you did great things with your community service project this fall at the Brookside Retirement Village?"

We half smiled. And possibly blushed.

"In fact, I know you did because I saw pictures of it in the front office!" She leaned in close. "Nice doggy wedding, by the way. . . ." Then she sat back up. "So you know what I'm thinking?"

We looked at each other and shrugged.

"I'm thinking that it might be up to *you* to make the Spring *Un*-Fair . . . well . . . fair again."

I turned around. I figured Principal Not-Such-A-Joy had walked into the room or something.

Principal Not-Such-A-Joy is our principal at Lakeview Elementary. Her real-alive name is Principal Joy.

Last year I organized a campaign to educate students about the importance of eating a well-rounded breakfast.

Only Principal Joy made me take down my posters because she said eating a well-rounded breakfast didn't mean eating only round things, like doughnuts.

I gave her a new name after that.

Principal Not-Such-A-Joy.

I turned around to check.

But no Principal Not-Such-A-Joy!

I did a scrunched-up face. "You mean us?" I said. "How?"

She smiled. "Something tells me if you can run a dog show, you'll come up with a plan for saving the Spring Fair." She winked at me. "And make it *fair* again." Then she held up the note. "Without passing notes while the teacher is talking, though," she said, staring at all of us. She looked outside at the playground. "In the meantime, I think you better run along. Recess is almost over."

Chapter 3

I STRAIGHTENED OUT MY TOWEL AND PATTED THE seat next to me.

"Here," I said when Heather got on the bus. "Sit here."

Bus seats are all crinkly and rippled. Like alligator skin. You never know if there might be a tooth or something stuck in them.

I use an Agnes-does-not-sit-on-bus-seats towel to protect myself.

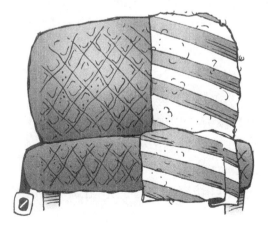

Emma scooted over and Heather sat down.

We were squeezed in tight like pieces of gum in a pack.

"She's got to be kidding, right?" Emma asked, putting her backpack on her lap. "What does Mrs. Carrick want us to do? Buy our own dunk tank or something?"

We'd told the rest of the club about Mrs. Carrick and her idea about saving the Spring Fair at the end of recess.

Emma had thought Mrs. Carrick was crazy.

Especially since the fair was only one week away!

Once we had settled into the seat, I cleared my throat. "Dear, dear young Emma," I said, patting her on her shoulder. "May I remind you that your presence at our last community service event was missed due to an unfortunately grave illness? 'Sick as a dog' I believe is how your mother described your condition, if I recall correctly."

Emma rolled her eyes.

I was using my best English accent.

I always use an English accent for club business, since it makes me sound more official.

It does *not*, as Fudgy says, make me sound as if I have a stuffy nose.

And I figured this was officially club business.

If anyone was going to save the Spring Fair, it was The Secret Knock Club! I was sure of it!

There was just one problem.

I had to convince everyone else!

"So?" Emma said, in not-a-good tone of voice. "What's that got to do with anything?"

"Now, now," I said slowly and Englishy. "Let's not get in a huff. I am merely saying that you were not fully aware of how well we Secret Knock types handled our last community service challenge. Rest assured that when we undertake the Spring *Un*-Fair, things will be no different."

Emma rolled her eyes again.

This time Heather did, too.

Fudgy looked over at us. "She's doing the accent again, isn't she?" He laughed. "What *is* it with the accent, Agnes?"

Heather leaned across the aisle. "Why yes she is, dear young Fudgy," she said, trying out an English accent of her own. Then she started laughing hysterically.

Laughing hysterically is when your whole body laughs.

Not just your mouth.

I reminded myself to put an X on the calendar for Heather when I got home!

We pulled up to my stop.

"Just meet me in my backyard in the clubhouse in an hour!" I said to everyone, grabbing my backpack. "We've got lots of

brain-hurricaning to do!"

Brain-hurricaning is just like brainstorming, only better. It's a top-of-the-line brainstorm!

And that's what we were going to need.

A top-of-the-line brainstorm!

If we were going to make the Spring *Un-Fair* fair again.

Chapter 4

"Got any coffee?" I asked Grandma Bling when I walked in the door. "I think it's going to be a long afternoon!"

Grandma Bling is my mom's mom. She lives with us now on account of Grandpa Hoover having a very bad case of being dead, although Grandma Bling says that's not a very nice way of saying it.

Grandma Bling is not her real-alive name. We call her that because she's got lots of sparkle and dazzle. She's like a Christmas tree full of ornaments that somebody forgot to take down.

Except she doesn't have a star on the top of her head. Unless you count her tiara. But she only wears that on BINGO night and when we play Room Service.

And here's the good news about Grandma Bling.

She's not a health nut like my mom.

She's a junk nut!

Although she has a rule: No coffee for nine-year-olds.

"Nope, no coffee," she said.

"How about a dunk tank then?" I answered. "I'll settle for a dunk tank."

She laughed and shook her head. Her earrings jingle-jangled back and forth. "Nope. Can't do that either, I'm afraid." She walked over to the refrigerator. "How about having a hop chocolate and tell me what's going on?"

Hop chocolate is one of Grandma Bling's specialties. It's just like *hot* chocolate, only the marshmallows are shaped like frogs.

And here's the rule: You have to stick your tongue out really far to lick the marshmallows off the top.

Grandma Bling is almost a professional on rules for drinks!

"So what's going on,

Agnes?" she asked, pouring the milk into the saucepan. She looked across the counter at me.

"Nothing," I said.

"Nothing?" She tilted her head, like she was trying to see if I looked better sideways. "What kind of nothing?"

There are two kinds of nothing in our house. The real nothing and the I-don't- want-to-talk-about-it-right-now kind of nothing.

This was the I-don't-want-to-talk-about-it-right-now kind.

She poured the hop chocolate into a mug.

"Well, whenever you're ready," she said, handing me the mug. "You know where I'll be."

Grandma Bling is not the knitting kind.

She's the watching-horse-racing-on-TV kind.

30

"Okay," I said. "And you know where I'll be, too." I grabbed my backpack and ran upstairs to Room 209. "Can you tell Mom where I am when she gets back from her yogurt class?" I yelled from the stop of the stairs.

"It's yoga, Agnes, *yoga*," I heard her say from the living room. I could tell she was making rearview mirror eyes. Rearview mirror eyes are the look she gives me in the car when I need to be more polite. Only sometimes she makes them in the living room. "But I'll be sure to tell her."

Room 209 is not my real-alive room number. Grandma Bling and I painted it on my door to make our house more "hotelish."

"Rat-A-Tat!" I called. "Where are you?"

I lifted up my bed shirt. "Here kitty kitty."

Bed *shirts* are just like bed*skirts*, only they're made out of your dad's old shirts.

Or at least mine is.

They're better 'cause of all the stuff you can put in the pockets!

I took out a cat treat.

"Here Rat-A-Tat!" I called again.

Rat-A-Tat is my thinking cat. Other people have thinking *caps*, but I have a thinking cat.

I sat on my floor in a yogurt pose and put my eye mask on my face and Rat-A-Tat on my head.

Yogurt poses make you look like a soft pretzel.

Only not as salty.

Then I closed my eyes and said *ummmm*, which is what all professional yogurt people say when they are trying to relax and think.

Only then Rat-A-Tat did a big meow.

Which is *not* what professional yogurt cats do when they are trying to help people named Agnes relax and think.

Grandma Bling knocked a little louder.

"Agnes?" she called out. "Yoo-hoo."

"Yes?" I said, trying to remain calm and yogurty. "Come in."

She opened the door.

"Heather's here," she said. "She says you're having a meeting today."

I jumped up uncalmly and unyogurtly.

"Heather?" I said, walking over to her before she could get very far into my room.

Because even though I was still mad about her fake English bus accent, I remembered something on my desk.

Something she might see!

I put Heather's arm through mine. "Come on," I said. "We don't want to be late for the meeting." I tapped my watch. "Gotta start these things on time, you know."

I threw my eye mask over my shoulder.
It landed on the X on my calendar.
The X by Heather's name.
The X that marked the spot.

Chapter 5

"THAT'S NOT *EXACTLY* RIGHT," I TOLD HEATHER from inside the clubhouse. "It's like this . . . tap, tap, tippity tap tap tap." I looked through the secret spy hole.

Heather was down on the ground tapping her secret knock.

"Try it again," I said.

She put her hands on her hips and started tapping her feet instead.

"No," I said, shaking my head. "That's still not it."

"Agnes, you know it's ME!" she yelled. "We just walked across your yard!"

"Okay, fine. Come in."

She climbed up the ladder and through the door that's in the floor. She looked down at her dress and started fluffing it.

Heather is always dressed fancy. Like you could maybe rent her for a wedding. "What was all *that* about?" she asked, still fluffing away.

I shrugged. "Nothing," I said.

It was the I-don't-want-to-talk-about-it-right-now kind of answer.

Plus, I'd decided not to stay mad at my X friend for long this time.

'Cause I needed her to help figure out how to get the dunk tank!

I started writing the agenda on the chalkboard.

"Here," I said, throwing Heather a piece of chalk. "Want to write the joke this time?"

We always make up a knock-knock joke for our meetings.

This is what Heather wrote:

Knock-Knock
Who's there?
Howie.
Howie who?
Howie gonna get a dunk tank?

It was *almost* like the knock-knock joke I made up when Heather and I weren't friends. Except the ending was a little different.

My joke went like this:

KNOCK-KNOCK
WHO'S THERE?
HOWIE.
HOWIE WHO?
HOWIE GONNA GET RID OF HEATHER?

Although I decided not to tell her that piece of information.

I just smiled and laughed at her joke.

"Hey, what's so funny up there?" Fudgy said from the ground. He started tapping the secret knock.

I tapped it back.

Which is what I do sometimes for security reasons.

"Enter," I said after the third knock.

"Here, take these." Fudgy reached up and handed me a plate of chocolate chip cookies. Then he climbed up the ladder.

"Ha, that's funny," he said, pointing to the board when he got in. "Good joke." He took back the plate of cookies and put one in his mouth.

Heather's face turned fluffy pink.

"Thanks," she said.

Just then Skipper, The Cape, and Emma showed up, too.

Heather's face turned back to fluffy white.

We were ready to start our meeting!

Everyone sat down on their beanbags.

"Okay, you know the rules," I said. "Write

down your ideas and we'll put them in here." I held up a bag. "We're going to pick the two best and then take a vote."

I crossed my fingers, toes, *and* eyes that my idea would win.

I passed out some paper and pencils and

we all started writing.

Except for Emma.

She didn't think we could raise enough money in time, so she wasn't going to brain-hurricane any ideas.

One by one everyone put their ideas in the bag when they were finished.

I held the bag up and shook it.

"Here goes," I said.

I reached in and pulled out the first idea.

IDEAS TO RENT A DUCK TANK, it said at the top.

There were no ideas underneath.

"A *DUCK* tank?" I said. "Let me guess."

I used my rolling eyes at The Cape.

The Cape is a not-so-good speller.

That's why we call him The Cape in the first place! Because one time in kindergarten he made a Super-Hero cape, only he spelled it with two p's, so guess what he was?

A *Supper*-Hero!

And then there was our last community service project when he made all the posters say COME AND SEE OUR PEST instead of COME AND SEE OUR PETS.

He laughed at his not-so-good spelling.

And then we all did, too.

"Next!" I said, reaching in for another piece of paper.

I unfolded the paper.

I could barely read anything on it. It was covered in chocolate smudges!

We all stared at Fudgy.

He looked down at his hands.

We looked over at the chocolate chip cookies.

"I couldn't help it," he said. "I'm really hungry."

"Well, do you want to tell us what it says?" I asked.

He licked his hands. "No. Not really," he said. "It wasn't very good anyway."

I shrugged. "Okay," I said.

I reached in the bag. AGAIN!

This time there weren't any words.

Just a picture.

Skipper started laughing.

"Don't you remember?" he asked.

I showed the picture around.

We all started laughing.

"Of course we do," I said. "It was the best part!"

Last year, Principal Not-Such-A-Joy's butt had a little "accident" in the dunk tank at the Spring Fair.

Principal Not-Such-A-Joy's butt is her dog, Trudy.

She's part beagle.

Part mutt.

She's a butt!

We gave the tank a new name after that.

The *stunk* tank!

"New rule," I said. "No butts in the tank this year."

"No butts!" everyone agreed.

But then I got a serious face.

We were down to two ideas!

Mine and Heather's.

I reached in the bag and pulled out my idea.

It was about doing a concert.

Heather's paper had a picture of two cupcakes on it.

She wanted to have a bake sale.

She called it a CupBake Sale.

It was time to vote.

This is how it worked: If we liked the idea, we put a check on it. If we didn't, we put an X.

It was kind of like my calendar.

I was crossing my fingers, toes, and eyes as everyone voted. Skipper stood up to count the votes.

He blew a huge bubble while he counted. He sucked it back up, like a vacuum cleaner, and then announced the winner. "Looks like this wins," he said.

I did a secret scream.

A secret scream is just like a regular scream, but only the inside of your body knows about it.

I smiled at the bubble letters in the middle of the paper.

Because I recognized those words: SECRET KNOCK ROCKS!

We were going to be in a band!

Chapter 6

TWO THINGS HAPPEN WHEN YOU'RE A ROCK STAR.

ONE: Your friends get mad at you because you don't ask them before you make yourself the lead singer of the band, and

TWO: You don't have time to do your homework.

I tried to tell Mrs. Carrick about the homework part the next day in class. Only she was busy being in a not-so-good mood with Fudgy, so I had to wait.

"Were there any super readers last night?" she asked at the start of class. I looked at her ice-cream hair again. It was held up with a giant clip that looked like a tarantula. Fudgy raised his hand super fast.

"Wonderful," Mrs. Carrick said, clapping her hands. "How much did you get through?"

Fudgy shrugged. "Almost the whole box," he said proudly.

Mrs. Carrick put her puzzled eyes on him. "Box?" she said. "For the super *reader* program?"

Fudgy's cheeks turned red. "Oh, I thought you said super *eater*."

I smiled.

Mrs. Carrick did not.

She made a "substitute face." Which is what substitutes do when they're thinking "I'm glad I'm not your real-alive teacher *all* the time!"

I raised my hand.

"Yes, Agnes?" she said, sounding hopeful. "Were *you* a super reader last night?"

I shook my head. "No, I'm sorry, Mrs. Carrick. I didn't have time to read last night. I was busy being a rock star."

Emma, The Cape, Fudgy, Skipper, and Heather all turned and looked at me.

"I'm sorry," Mrs. Carrick said. "Did I just hear you correctly? Did you say you were busy being a *rock star*?"

"That's right," I said, kicking my rock star cowgirl boots out into the aisle. "But don't worry. You haven't missed out. I'll be signing autographs after the concert." I stood up and

walked toward her desk. I smoothed out my leather jacket on the way. "In the meantime," I said, "here's a note about my homework."

Mrs. Carrick shook her head and put on her glasses that do not jump.

Then she read the note:

Dear Mrs. Substitute Whose Name is NOT Carrot:

Sorry Agnes did not do her homework last night. Come to think of it, sorry she won't be doing it at all this week. She is very busy being a rock star. When you're a rock star, you have to do hair. And makeup. And pick out clothes. And get tattoos.

Well, sometimes you don't get tattoos.

But it still takes a lot of time.

So that's why Agnes won't be doing regular boring stuff like homework this week.

See you at the concert!
Rock on,
    Agnes

Mrs. Carrick put down the note and cleared her throat. "Rock Star? Concert?"

she said. "Have I missed something?"

"Nope, not yet," I said, smiling. "The concert's not until next weekend."

"I'm sorry, Agnes, but since when did you become a rock star?" she asked. She looked quite pale.

"Since you told me to," I said.

"Since *I* told you to?" She grew even paler. "When was that?"

"Well, you didn't tell me to become a rock star exactly. But you did say to figure out a way to make the Spring *Un*-fair fair again, so that's what I did. . . . I mean *we* did. . . ." I looked around at the rest of the club.

They were glaring at me.

I ignored them.

"We voted to have a concert to raise money to rent the dunk tank for the Spring Fair," I continued. "So, that's what we're doing. Next weekend. In my backyard. *That's* why I'm a rock star!"

Mrs. Carrick looked at the rest of the kids in the club.

"But why aren't *they* dressed like you?" she said, pointing to them. "Aren't they going to be in the concert, too?"

I turned around and looked at everybody.

Then I leaned in real close to Mrs. Carrick's desk. "Yeah, but they're not the lead singer," I said. "Only the lead singer gets to dress like this." I patted my leather jacket.

Mrs. Carrick looked at the rest of the club again. "Oh, I guess you voted on that, too, huh?" she asked. "How exciting!"

My face turned red, like somebody was adding Kool-Aid to it.

"Well, not *exactly*," I whispered.

Chapter 7

"Close your eyes, Grandma," I said, walking through the front door after I got off the bus.

Grandma Bling was in the kitchen marrying the steak for dinner.

"Yum, yum, yum!" I said. "What are you marrying it with this time?"

Grandma Bling laughed. "It's called *marinating*, Agnes. And I'm just using a little salt and pepper and olive oil. Your favorite."

Which was true.

Grandma Bling's steak was always my favorite. My mom makes steak, too, only when she makes it, it's so tough and chewy, we don't call it steak.

We call it mis-steak.

Grandma Bling put the steak down and washed her hands.

"Now what was that about closing my eyes?" She dried her hands and put them over her eyes. "Do you have a surprise for me, Agnes?" She peeked through her fingers and winked. "You know how I love surprises!"

I nodded. "Sure do," I said. "I think you'll

be *very* surprised." I took off her scarf and wrapped it around her head for extra eyeball security.

She looked like a Grandma Bling mummy!

"Okay," she said. "I'm ready."

"Me too," I said.

I took a deep breath and started singing.

"Oh, dear," Grandma Bling said, interrupting me. "Is that Rat-A-Tat? I thought she was outside." She tapped the counter. "Here kitty, kitty!" she called. "Come and wait with Grandma for our surprise!"

I did a scrunched-up, mad face at Mummy Bling.

Even though she couldn't see it.

"Grandma!!!" I shouted.

"I'm still waiting," she said. Her arms were stretched out. Like she really *was* a mummy.

"Grandma, that *was* the surprise."

"What was?" She un-mummied herself and looked around.

"Me! Singing!"

She unwound her scarf and laid it on the counter. "Oh, that was you singing?" She made an oops face. "I guess I must not have heard you very well with that thing wrapped around my head. Let's try it again, okay?" She headed for the sink. "How about some water first? That might help you clear your throat."

"Okay," I said. "But none of that tap stuff. I only drink bottled now. It's what all the stars do."

Grandma Bling ignored me. "I'm ready," she said.

I started singing.

Her eyes got bigger and bigger, like somebody was blowing them up for a party.

"Well?" I asked, when I finished. "What do you think?"

Her eyes stayed large and blown-up.

Her mouth started to move. But slowly, like it didn't want to get a ticket for going too fast. "Well, I think we all have different talents, Agnes," she said. She patted me on the shoulder. "Maybe . . . maybe singing's just not one of yours."

"Not one of mine!" I stepped back. "But it has to be. I've made myself the lead singer of the band!!" I looked down at my clothes. "See?"

I was wearing my rock-star cowgirl boots, ripped tights, a skirt, and a leather jacket. Underneath was my T-shirt. It said BORN TO ROCK.

Grandma Bling shook her head and went to answer the phone.

"Yes, she's here," I heard her say. She turned around and held out the phone.

"It's Heather. She wants to talk to you"— she covered the mouthpiece—"about this lead singer thing, I think."

I slumped my rock-star shoulders and took the phone.

Grandma Bling gave me a look. A whatever-you-need-to-do-to-make-it-better look. Then she walked out of the kitchen.

I took the phone.

Heather started talking. She didn't sound as angry as I thought she would. "We're not mad anymore that you made yourself the lead singer without asking us," she said.

I made curious eyes at the phone.

"Really?" I answered.

"Yeah, nobody else wants to do it, anyway," she said.

"They don't?"

"No way! Turns out everyone stares at you when you're the lead singer."

"Oh," I said.

"And if you mess up, they laugh at you."

I gulped.

"And the worst part is . . . sometimes, if you're really bad, they throw stuff at you. Like rotten tomatoes. Fudgy told us everything. He asked Reggie."

Reggie is Fudgy's older brother. He's in high school. He's the lead singer of a band called Smashing Good.

He should know.

I put the phone down and took a sip of my un-rock-star tap water.

"So the job's all yours," I heard her say through the phone.

Chapter 8

I HUNG UP THE PHONE AND CALLED FUDGY'S house on the dot!

I always call people on the dot.

This time I'd chosen a tan one. Our kitchen floor is covered with green and tan dots, so I always stand on one when I make calls.

Especially official club business ones.

But then Grandma Bling came back into the kitchen.

So I moved into the pantry, where I would have more privacy.

And better snacks.

"May I please speak with Reginald Harris?" I asked in a professional, rock-star voice.

I decided to use a professional, rock-star voice and not my English accent this time.

"Reginald Harris?" Fudgy said, laughing.

"Are you kidding, Agnes? What are you calling him that for? Anyway, I think *Reggie*'s busy. He's in the garage with Smashing Good, practicing."

I figured "Reginald" could at least give me some professional, rock-star advice.

Like how to get tomato stains out of leather.

Reggie looks just like Fudgy, only he's really tall and skinny. He's like a stretched-out-piece-of-gum version of Fudgy.

This is how all the guys in Smashing Good dress: in black.

Black boots.

Black pants.

Black T-shirts.

That way they blend into the dark when people try to throw tomatoes at them, probably.

"What's going on, Agnes?" Fudgy asked. I could tell he was chewing on something. He swallowed. "What do you want to talk to him for, anyway?"

"You wouldn't understand," I said. "It's rock-star stuff. Just go get him, would you?"

"Rock-star stuff? You're really going to do that?" He laughed. "Didn't you talk to Heather? Well, good luck. I'm sticking to the drums. Reggie said I could borrow one of the band's old sets."

"Good. That's great. Now go get him, would you?"

"Okay," Fudgy said. "But I'm warning you. He doesn't like to be disturbed when he's practicing."

I thought fast. "No problem," I said. "I've got it under control."

I grabbed a piece of paper and put a pen in my hair.

"Good afternoon, Mr. Reginald Harris," I said politely when Reggie got on the phone. I was using my best newspaper reporter voice.

"Who's this?" Reggie said. I could hear music in the background. "Speak up. I can't hear you too good."

"This is Cornelia"—I quickly looked around the pantry—"Cornelia Nabisco," I said.

And suddenly I realized that Heather has a pantry name, too.

Heather *Kellogg*!

"What do you want, Miss *Nabisco*?" Reggie said. "I'm kind of busy."

"I am calling from the *Highland Paper News Reporting Post Times Gazette*," I said,

59

quickly making up a non-pantry name. "And we are asking all area rock stars a very important question today."

Reggie laughed. "Oh yeah? What's that?"

"First off, let me start by asking if you've had any good wigs lately."

"Wigs?" Reggie asked.

I shook my head. "I mean jigs. Jigs! Have you played any good jigs lately?"

"You mean *gigs*?" Reggie asked, still laughing. "Where are you calling from again?"

"Yeah, that's it! *Gigs!*" I said. I had pantry brain! "Have you had any good *gigs* lately?"

Reggie thought for a minute. "No, not really," he said. "Just at the old folks' home last weekend. . . ."

"The Brookside Retirement Village?" I said, in an un-reporter voice. "We . . . I mean . . . never mind." I shook my head and came out of the pantry. On account of my sugar fog brain!

Grandma Bling stared at me.

"We did have something scheduled for next Saturday, but it just fell through," Reggie said.

"That's a shame," I said. "I hear there's going to be some really great talent playing in the area on Saturday."

"Oh yeah?" Reggie said. "Who?"

I paused. "Ummm . . . you probably haven't heard of them. They're an up-and-coming band."

Reggie laughed.

"Well, do you think they're *up* to *coming* to our garage to get some tips before their big show, *Agnes*?" he asked. "Fudgy told me all about you making yourself the lead singer. He thought you might need some . . . well . . . help."

My reporter days were over!

I pulled the pen out of my hair.

"Sure," I said, blushing. "Let me call the other club members and tell them to meet me there. Tell Fudgy we'll be on our way."

Chapter 9

GARAGES ARE GOOD FOR THREE THINGS.

Car stuff.

Stinky garbage stuff.

And rock-star stuff.

We were there for the rock-star stuff.

I looked around the place.

The walls were covered with posters of famous singing people.

Only guess what?

No tomatoes on those people!

Just tattoos.

And big, thick chains around their necks.

And piercings everywhere that made them look like they had the chicken pox.

Heather made an ewww face at the posters. She grabbed The Cape's arm.

Even though he wasn't a real Super-Hero.

I did a pretend smile.

A pretend smile is just like a regular smile, only you don't mean it on the inside.

"I like what you've done with the place," I said, nodding my head slowly.

Reggie stopped tuning his guitar.

"Cool," he said.

The rest of Smashing Good nodded at us.

"Hey," they said.

Rock-star people sometimes only say one word at a time.

To save energy for their concerts, probably.

Reggie put his guitar down. He walked over to Fudgy and noodled his head. "So, my little Fudger's going to be in a band, is he?" he said. He looked around at the rest of

Smashing Good. "Cool."

He squeezed "Fudger's" cheeks.

Fudger turned Twizzler red.

"Now let's get ready to rock 'n' roll," Reggie said. He threw Fudgy a set of drumsticks. "Let's see what you've got, little Bro."

Fudgy looked like the only place he wanted to roll was out the door!

He wasn't used to drumsticks.

The kind of drumstick Fudgy is used to.

The kind of drumsticks Fudgy is NOT used to.

Unless they were the chicken kind.

He looked scared. Kind of like Heather still did.

"Just don't break anything," Reggie said. He sat down on a paint can to watch the show. "Deal?"

Fudgy didn't move.

"Well?" Reggie said, tapping his feet. "We don't have all day, you know." He looked around. "What about you, Cape Boy?" he said, pointing to The Cape. "You want to give it a try?"

The Cape always wears his cape on special occasions.

This time he wore it with very un-rock pajama pants.

The Cape didn't answer.

Reggie turned to me. "Okay, what about you . . . Miss . . . *Nabisco*, was it? You want to give it a try?"

I missed my pantry reporter days!

"Okay," I said, walking over to the microphone stand. "I guess."

I used my wobbly legs to get there.

I reached for the microphone. It was too

high up. Like a giraffe's neck.

Reggie walked over to help.

He took the microphone off the stand. "Here," he said, handing it to me. "Let's hear what you've got."

And guess what?

Turns out you can have stage fright even without a stage!

It's called garage fright.

I looked at Smashing Good.

And Heather.

And Fudgy.

And the rest of The Secret Knock Club.

They were all staring at me, like I was a bug under a microscope.

I crossed my legs and jumped up and down a little bit.

Because garage fright can make you have to go to the bathroom.

"Let's hear it," Reggie said again. "After all, if you're going to be the lead singer . . ."

I put the microphone down.

"Yeah, about that," I said. "I guess I was wrong to make myself the lead singer without asking anyone." I looked down at the ground.

"Even though I do look *really* good in these boots." Everyone was still staring at me. "So, if anyone else wants the job . . ."

Reggie looked around the garage.

He shrugged. "Looks like there aren't any takers," he said. He leaned in close to me. "Take a deep breath," he said. "You'll be fine. Promise."

I stared at everyone.

"On the count of three," Reggie said. "One. Two. Three."

And I sang.

Even though it sounded a bit more like

croaking.

I stopped croaking.

"I can't do it!" I said, running out of the garage. "I can't sing!"

And The Secret Knock Club learned a new secret that day.

That Agnes Mary Murphy, the lead singer of the band, doesn't have a good voice.

Except for when she's saying "THE CONCERT IS CANCELED!"

Chapter 10

THE NEXT DAY AT SCHOOL, MRS. CARRICK CALLED us up to her desk before class started. "How are the plans for the fair coming along?" she asked.

Mrs. Carrick had a first-thing-in-the-morning smile on her face.

They're what teachers have before the day "sucks them dry," as Mrs. Duncan, our real-alive teacher, says.

We looked at one another.

"It's still unfair," we all agreed.

"But I thought you were having a concert to raise money?" She looked at her calendar. "In fact, your concert's this weekend, isn't it?" She started nodding. "Yes, yes, I knew I marked it down." She pointed to Saturday. "Only two days away! Wouldn't want to miss that!"

"Oh yes you would," I said, under my breath.

"What was that, Agnes?" Mrs. Carrick said.

I made a puppy dog head. Puppy dog heads are when you hang your head down to the ground, but your eyeballs are still looking up.

Only without the drool.

I told her the truth. "There's not going to be a concert after all," I said. Okay, maybe not the *whole* truth. "It's been canceled . . . due to . . ." I looked around the room. I saw Mrs. Duncan's weather chart. "Due to bad weather."

Mrs. Carrick looked surprised. "Bad weather? But we're having a heat wave!"

I thought about that news.

"Yes, but heat can be very bad for concert people. Imagine what it would do to your ice-cream hair if you came and watched." I smiled. "We are only thinking of others. . . ."

"Ice-cream hair?" Mrs. Carrick said. "Should I even ask?"

I shook my head and changed the subject.

"Actually . . . it's canceled because of Emma."

Even Emma looked surprised by that news.

"Emma?" Mrs. Carrick asked. "Why are you canceling it because of Emma?"

"Just look at her!" I said.

Mrs. Carrick put on her glasses. She stretched her neck to get a better look at Emma. "She looks perfectly fine to me," she said.

"Well, maybe *now*," I said. "But I'm sure something's coming." I leaned in close to Mrs. Carrick. "She has a habit of being sick for community service projects. We should cancel it now to protect everyone. . . ."

"Protect them from what?" Mrs. Carrick asked.

I turned and looked at Emma.

"Look," I said, pointing to her face. "Could be the start of the chicken pox."

Emma put her hands up to her face. "What?" she screamed.

"Or the start of *freckles*," said Mrs. Carrick.

"Okay, well what about the pink eye?" I said. "I hear that stuff's *very* contagious."

"Pink eye?" Mrs. Carrick just shook her head.

"It could just be starting," I pointed out. "It might be *light pink* eye right now." I smiled. "That's why you can't see it yet. . . ."

"Bad weather? Chicken pox? Light pink eye? Why don't you tell me what's going on, Agnes? Why don't you want to have the concert?"

I scrunched my eyes to make it look as if I could possibly have light pink eye, too.

You never know.

Then I leaned across Mrs. Carrick's desk. "I have garage fright," I whispered.

"Garage fright?" she whispered back.

As usual, I had to explain.

"It's just like stage fright," I said, still whispering. "Only you can get it in a garage, too."

She thought for a minute.

"You mean you're *afraid* to sing, or you just *can't* sing?"

I thought for a minute, too. "Ummm . . . well, I'm not *exactly* sure. It's hard to tell. Maybe both?"

She grabbed a notebook. "I have the perfect solution," she said. She wrote something down. "Here," she said, handing me the note. It looked like a prescription. "Go and see Mrs. Roman during recess. I'm sure she'll be able to help. Trust me, there won't be any need to cancel the concert after you work with her for a little while!"

I looked down at the note.

Sure enough.

It said Mrs. Roman.

The music teacher!

Chapter 11

T<small>AP</small>, <small>TAP</small>, <small>TAP</small>!!!

I knocked on Mrs. Roman's door very musically.

Because I am almost a professional knocker from The Secret Knock Club, that's why.

Mrs. Roman opened the door.

"Here." I handed her my note. "This is what I'm here for," I said.

I am not sure, but this is probably what the note said:

Please, please, please teach Agnes to sing and get over her garage fright so she can do the concert and I can live an easier life. After all, I am not her real-alive teacher, so I am not used to all these shenanigans.

Beggingly,
Mrs. Carrick
(the one who can't handle much more)

P.S. If you get a chance, please ask Agnes what she means by ice-cream hair. I'd love to know!

Or something like that. . . .

Mrs. Roman read the note. And here's the good thing: She did not ask me what ice-cream hair was.

"I have an idea," she said. "I think it will really help." She put the note down and took off her scarf.

And here's something I learned about Mrs. Roman that day.

She *does* have a neck!

I never really knew 'cause she always wears scarves. That woman looks like she's been in a permanent car accident.

And here's something else I learned about Mrs. Roman.

She blindfolds kids.

Or at least ones that have garage fright.

She wrapped her scarf around and around my head.

It was a zebra print one.

The scarf.

Not my head.

Suddenly I looked like I had been in a car accident, too!

Only a bit higher up.

"Where's the piñata?" I asked, reaching out my hands to feel around.

"There's no piñata," Mrs. Roman said. "Take a deep breath," she said, slowly and calmly, like we were in a yogurt class.

But here's the thing: It's hard to breathe deeply when you have a zebra head.

"I can't breathe!" I started panicking. "I can't breathe!" My legs started moving back and forth, like they were trying to breathe for my mouth.

Mrs. Roman lifted up my zebraness. "Agnes, it's not covering your *mouth*." We were eyeball to eyeball.

"You can breathe," she said. "What I want you to do is sing without seeing anything or anyone."

"Does a zebra count?"

Mrs. Roman pretended she hadn't heard.

"Close your eyes, Agnes, and sing without an audience." She paused. "You'll be amazed how much it frees you to sing to your true potential!"

I sang.

'Cause what choice do you have when your teacher has you zebra-blindfolded?

"La, la, la, la, la," I started. I peeked out. Mrs. Roman was smiling. "And again," she said. She waved her hands back and forth to the music.

"Round two," I said. "Coming up."

"La, la, la, la, la," I sang again. Only this time my voice was higher. And louder.

And guess what?

Scarves really *do* help you sing!

Maybe that's why Mrs. Roman wears one every day.

She picked up a tambourine. She shook it in rhythm to my singing. My talented, rock-star-scarf singing.

I could hear her dancing around the room with that tambourine. I imagined her dress flowing up and down, like it wanted in on the action, too.

And suddenly I didn't have any kind of fright.

Stage. Garage. *Or* blindfold.

I was free to be a singer! I was free to be Agnes, the rock star.

Only there was just one problem.

"May I borrow this?" I asked, pointing to Mrs. Roman's scarf. "My rock starness depends on it."

She laughed. "It's all yours," she said.

I said good-bye and thank you to Mrs. Roman.

And her neck.

And I clickity-clacked my boots right out of her room.

The concert was back on!

Chapter 12

HERE'S THE BAD THING ABOUT BEING A TALENTED, blindfolded singer.

Lots of bruises.

I learned that on the bus in the afternoon.

"Watch it!"

"Ouch!"

"Get out of my way!"

"What do you think you're doing?"

But I didn't mind.

There's a price to pay for fame.

Regular, non-rock-star people wouldn't understand.

"You're still wearing that thing?" Fudgy asked, when I finally made it to the back of the bus. "What did Mrs. Roman do to you?"

"Quiet," Emma said, ssh-ing him. "She's in her zone."

I tried to sit down.

"Her zone?" Fudgy yelled. "Are you kidding me? It's more like my lap!" He gave my backpack a push.

Emma helped me into the seat across from Fudgy.

"Really, Agnes," he said. "Why *are* you still wearing that? You look ridiculous."

I couldn't admit I didn't think I could sing without it. And Mrs. Roman said I needed lots of practice.

"It's my signature," I said, adjusting the knot.

"Your what?"

"My signature," I said. "You know. As a singer. Every singer has one. Some have tattoos. Some have chains." I patted my head. "*I* have a scarf."

"Oh, brother," Fudgy said. "So you're what? The lead *scarf* singer?"

I turned to Emma.

At least I think I did.

"Can you tell everyone to meet in the clubhouse in half an hour?" I asked. "We've got lots of practicing to do now that the concert is back on."

"Why couldn't you just tell us that yourself?" Fudgy asked. "We're right here. We heard everything you just said, Agnes."

I sat up in my seat.

"I have people for that now," I said.

"You have *what*?" Fudgy asked.

"You know. People."

"*People?*"

"Yes, all the big stars have them." I fixed my scarf. "You know. People to do stuff for you. Make important announcements. Get your water. Make sure you have snacks. Iron your clothes. That kind of thing."

"Iron your clothes?" Fudgy *and* Emma sounded surprised.

"Oh brother," Fudgy said. "I think I liked it better when the concert was canceled."

"Well, Emma's okay with it, so that's all that really matters," I said.

Emma didn't answer.

"Right, Emma?"

Fudgy laughed. "Hey, don't look now, but I think your *people* just got off the bus!"

I pulled up my scarf and looked out the window. I opened it. "Don't forget. The clubhouse. Half an hour!"

"I think you might need to get new people," Fudgy said, laughing.

My zebra head and I ignored him the rest of the ride.

Later on we were all in the clubhouse. "Practice makes perfect!" I said as I started singing for everyone. "Mrs. Roman said so."

"Really?" Fudgy asked. "Practice makes *me* want to plug my ears!" Skipper and The Cape laughed.

I lifted up my scarf.

So my eyes could do their thing for a minute.

And I stared at Fudgy.

It was a good and strong stare, too.

'Cause my eyes hadn't been used in a while.

I started singing again and put my scarf back down. "La la la la la!" My voice went up and down like a yo-yo. "That's just a little warm-up trick Mrs. Roman taught me," I said to everyone. "You might not have heard about it before. All lead singers do it."

I sang a few more notes and put my hands on my neck.

"Water!" I shouted. "I need water!"

And, okay, maybe I clapped my hands, too.

Heather walked over with the water.

"Looks like she's got new *people*," I heard Fudgy say to Skipper. They both laughed.

I looked at the bottle. "Is it bubbly?" I asked. "I really prefer bubbly nowadays."My people looked at me with you're-pushing-your-luck faces.

I continued singing.

Until my throat felt kind of dry again.

I stopped and sat down on my beanbag.

"Can you bring me the list?" I asked Heather. "It should be on the agenda board." She walked over and grabbed the list I'd made of everyone's responsibilities. I smiled as she walked back to me. "You're such a doll," I said, smiling.

This is called keeping your people happy.

"And while you're at it," I added, "can you bring me some of those M&M's? Only the red ones, though. I only do red now."

Heather did red, too.

A red, mad face!

I looked down at the list. "Let's see," I said. "Who's doing what at the concert?"

"I'm selling tickets," The Cape said, raising his hand.

"I'm playing the tambourine," Heather said.

"Drums!" Fudgy called out. "I'm playing the drums. Reggie said I could practice tonight."

"Great," I said. I crossed off their names.

"Emma? What about you? Anything?"

Emma shook her head. "I guess I'll just help The Cape with the tickets."

I looked at Emma. "Are you sure? You know you don't have to be embarrassed if you don't have a real talent. You could always be a backup singer. You don't even have to know all the words for that. You can just hum if you want."

"No thanks!" Emma said, all huffy. "I'll just stick to the tickets."

"Okay, that just leaves you, then, Skipper," I said, turning to him. "What are you going to do?" He was sitting on his beanbag. He thought for a minute. "I've got a harmonica at home," he said. "I guess I could play that."

"Sounds good!" I crossed Skipper's name off, too. Then I looked back down at the list to find my name. "And I'm . . ."

"We know! We know!" everyone said, all at once. "You're the lead singer." And I sang a little extra tune for that good news.

Chapter 13

"Good Morning Lakeview Elementary students. Rock on!" I said into the microphone.

Principal Not-Such-A-Joy had agreed to let us announce our concert during the morning announcements on Friday. The day before the concert!

We were in the front office.

Behind us was the picture of Principal Not-Such-A-Joy's butt getting married.

I was wearing my rock-star cowgirl boots again.

And this time I had piercings, too.

Just Married!

Well, okay, I had bedazzled jewels where I *would* have piercings.

If I was allowed to get them.

And if I didn't faint at the sight of needles.

"It's The Secret Knock Club here," I continued. "Come out tomorrow and help us raise money for a dunk tank to make the Spring *Un*-Fair *fair* again. Sit back, relax, and listen as The Secret Knock Club Rocks . . . my backyard!" I held up a picture of my rock-star self.

Principal Not-Such-A-Joy came over.

"Honey, it's a loudspeaker," she whispered. "They can't see that."

"Oh, right," I said out loud. "Make that Agnes's backyard. Tomorrow at two. Free to get in. A dollar to stay. Be there and get your dunk on!"

I stopped and cleared my throat.

It felt kind of funny.

Like it was scratchy.

Fudgy grabbed the microphone.

"We're selling snacks, too!" he said. "Just in

case the concert's a bust."

I glared at him.

'Cause of my no-zebra head, that's why.

I had taken off my scarf because I needed my eyeballs that morning.

"You never know," he said, looking at me.

I put my hand over the microphone. "First of all," I said, "you're in my personal space." I shooed him away, like he was a bad smell. "Rock stars don't like to be crowded. And second of all, my scarf and I have it all under control. There's *nothing* to worry about."

I started talking into the microphone again. "Rock on!" I said. "See you all tomorrow. Peace out!"

"Peace out?" Fudgy asked. "Is that another one of those things *rock stars* say?" He shook his head. "You're too much, Agnes."

I know a compliment when I hear one!

"Thank you very much," I said. "Now, let's go, you guys. Mrs. Roman said we could use her room to practice. She doesn't have a class until eleven. And Mrs. Carrick said it was okay to miss language arts just this once." I grabbed Emma and Heather by their arms and we walked fast . . . okay, *ran* down the hall.

"Cool," Fudgy said when he walked in the room. Mrs. Roman had a set of drums, a tambourine, a harmonica, and a microphone ready for us.

She looked up from her desk.

"Come in. Come in," she said. Then she put her hands up to her neck.

"It's okay," I said. "I don't need to borrow it." I pulled out her zebra scarf. "I have this one, remember?"

"How could I forget?" she asked.

She took the scarf and helped me tie it around my head.

"Now. Remember what I said yesterday, Agnes. Practice makes . . . ?"

"It makes us miss language arts!" Skipper said.

"Now, now, boys," Mrs. Roman said. "I'll ask again. Practice makes . . . ?"

"Perfect!" I said back.

"Yeah, right," Fudgy said under his breath.

"I'm sorry, Fudgy," said Mrs. Roman. "Did you have something to say?"

Fudgy thought for a second. "I said . . . that's right, Mrs. Roman. That's absolutely right!"

"Good," she said. "And since you agree so much, why don't you take a crack at those," she said, pointing to the drums. She handed him the drumsticks.

Fudgy gulped.

And he played the drums.

But not so perfectly!

Mrs. Roman walked over to him.

She whispered something to Fudgy.

He whispered something back and pointed to all of us.

She chuckled. "Somebody else I know has that problem, too," she said, taking off her scarf. "Maybe you should call yourselves The Secret *Scarf* Club instead!"

And she wrapped her scarf around Fudgy's head.

The pink, flowery one that matched her bright pink dress.

And guess what?

Scarves aren't just good for singing.

They're good for drumming, too.

Even pink, flowery ones.

Chapter 14

SOMETIMES SCARF-WEARING MUSIC TEACHERS aren't right.

Practice does *not* always make perfect.

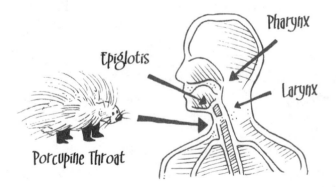

Porcupine Throat

Epiglotis

Pharynx

Larynx

Sometimes it makes porcupine throat!

Porcupine throat is when your throat is scratchy.

And prickly.

And pokey.

And doesn't work.

It is *not in any way* good for talented rock-star singers.

I discovered it when I woke up that morning. The morning of the concert!

I went through my list.

Scarf?

Check.

Rock-star outfit?

Check.

Cowgirl boots?

Check.

Tattoo?

In my dreams.

And then I discovered something was missing.

MY VOICE!

I screamed.

Only it was an inside scream, on account of the not-so-good-of-a voice and all.

I'd la-la-la-ed my voice away!

I grabbed a pencil and paper and wrote:

WANTED:

One lead-singing rock star.
Available for afternoon hours. As in
TODAY's afternoon.
**Must love scarves. **
Knowledge of removing tomato
stains a plus.
Real-alive lead singer would do
the job, only she's come down with
a rare and unfortunate condition.
Okay, she's lost her voice. But could
turn worse any minute! Interested?
Call my house IMMEDIATELY RIGHT
NOW. Actually, don't bother to call.
Just show up. Agnes's backyard. 1:30
to warm up. 2:00 for the show.

I looked at the ad.

"Who am I kidding?" I thought to myself.
"It's too late to find anyone."

I ripped the ad to pieces and ran downstairs.

Grandma Bling and my dad were drinking
coffee.

Mom was taking a batch of cookies out of
the oven.

They all looked up.

"There's our girl," Dad said, smiling. "Our
little rock star! Ready for your big day?"

"Uhhh . . ." I whispered in a very prickly,

pokey, porcupine whisper.

Grandma Bling looked at me. "Why are you whispering like that, Agnes?" She sipped her coffee. "Oh, I get it! You're trying to save your voice for this afternoon." She winked at my mom. "That's very smart of her! I hear all the big names do that before shows."

They both smiled.

I smiled back.

Only mine was a pretend smile.

I didn't know what to say. I didn't want to disappoint anyone.

Mom put the cookies on the counter.

"There," she said, counting. "That makes twelve dozen so far. I'd say you could sell two for twenty-five cents. That'll definitely help get you on your way to that dunk tank. What did Ted at The Prop Shop say he'd rent it to you for? He's giving you a discount, right? Fifty dollars since the fair's such a great community event?"

"And Fudgy's still bringing all the other snacks, right, Agnes?" Grandma Bling asked. She looked around the place. "I think you'll have plenty of food."

"Ummm . . ." I whispered. I started to tell them what had happened.

"Oh, dear, don't strain your voice!" Grandma Bling said. She started putting the cookies in bags. Her shoulders went up and down. "This is *so* exciting!"

I nodded.

'Cause that's all you can do when you have porcupine throat.

Then I ran out of the kitchen and grabbed some poster board.

Out in the backyard I put up a sign on the fence.

And then I put my scarf around my eyes. And tied it really tight.

To help suck up the zebra tears.

Chapter 15

"Hey, where do you want these?"

I took off my wet scarf.

And used my wet eyeballs to see.

And there were Fudgy and Heather.

Reggie and the rest of Smashing Good were standing behind them.

They were holding a bunch of snacks.

I wiped my eyes.

"Reggie and the guys helped us carry them

over," Fudgy said. He leaned in close. "Truth is, I think they just want to see the concert."

I gulped.

Reggie spoke.

"Yo," he said.

He was doing his one-word, rock-star thing.

I didn't answer.

I was doing my no-word, porcupine-throat thing.

I couldn't even whisper now. My voice was officially zippo!

Fudgy stood there for a minute. "Well?" he asked again. "They're getting kind of heavy here."

I still didn't answer.

Fudgy got huffy. "You know this diva thing is getting old, Agnes." He turned to Heather. "Don't you think?" He shook his head. "I mean, *now* what? You can't even talk to us?"

He bent down to leave the snacks in the driveway. "We'll be back in a little bit after we get the drums. Maybe you'll be able to talk to us by the time we get back." He turned to Reggie. "Come on, guys."

Heather looked at me.

I shrugged.

And that's when I did what anyone without a voice would do.

I kicked the fence.

Really hard.

Because my *feet* still worked!

Fudgy and the rest of Smashing Good turned around.

Heather's eyes got big.

I did an inside scream and pointed to the fence.

"Canceled?" they read. "Due to technical difficulties?"

"Not again!" Fudgy said. "How many times is this thing going to be canceled?" He looked around. "Anyway, *what* technical difficulties?"

I pointed to my throat.

Then I took the marker out of my pocket and added the word *voice* to the sign.

"You mean you lost your voice?" Heather said. *"That's* why you're not talking?"

Fudgy looked at me. "Why didn't you say so!"

I pointed to my throat again.

"Oh, yeah," he said, nodding.

I took the marker out one more time.

"What are we going to do about the concert?" I wrote on the sign.

Heather took the marker. "I don't know," she wrote. "Any ideas?"

And suddenly I had one!

I looked across the driveway.

And pointed . . .

to Reggie!

Chapter 16

"PLEASE? PLEASE? PLEASE? PLEASE?"
Fudgy asked Reggie. "Will you do it,
PLEEEASE?" He was using his begging voice.

Reggie looked at me.

I got down on the ground.

I was using my begging hands.

And my begging knees.

Which did not mean I was asking him to
marry me.

Skipper, The Cape, and Emma showed up
just in time.

To get in on the begging, too.

PLEASE! PLEASE! PLEASE! PLEASE!

"Hey what are we begging for, anyway?"
Skipper asked, halfway through. Fudgy leaned
over to him. "For Reggie to sing," he said.

"Reggie?" Skipper said. "Why Reggie? What about Agnes?" He pointed to me.

"She can't sing," Fudgy said. "She's lost it."

Skipper nodded. "Tell me about it. You know what she asked me to do for her yesterday?"

And here's the thing about not having a voice.

You can't scream at people!

Fudgy shook his head. "No, I mean her voice. She's lost her voice."

I smirked at Skipper.

"Agnes can't sing," Fudgy said. "We need Reggie and the guys to help if there's gonna be a concert today."

We all looked at Reggie.

He turned to the rest of Smashing Good and shrugged. They nodded.

Then Reggie did his one-word talking.

And guess what?

It wasn't the no word.

It was the yes one.

The concert was back on!

AGAIN.

We had lots to do.

Reggie threw the keys to the Smashing Good guys. "Here, take these and go and get the drums." He turned to Fudgy. "We're still going to get little Fudger onstage to help out, right?"

Little Fudger gulped. "I guess," he said. He looked scared. He looked at me. I nodded and pointed to my scarf. My lucky zebra one. Fudgy reached into his pocket and pulled out his lucky scarf. His pink, flowery one. "Sure," he said, rubbing his scarf like a baby blanket. "I'll do it."

Just then Mom and Dad and Grandma Bling walked outside.

They looked surprised to see Reggie.

Reggie stopped setting up the snacks and explained everything to them.

They all gave me a big hug.

A big I'm-sorry-you-can't-be-a-talented-scarf-wearing-lead-singer-today hug.

I gave them a big hug right back.

Because here's the thing.

Your arms still work even if your mouth doesn't.

And besides, one way or another we still needed to raise money for that dunk tank! We still needed to make the Spring Un-Fair fair again.

We all started working.

Grandma Bling helped Reggie with the snacks.

Mom ran back inside and brought out the cookies she'd made.

Dad helped run some electrical wires.

Emma and The Cape helped set up the ticket booth.

And Skipper, Fudgy, and Heather practiced, practiced, practiced.

Pretty soon the backyard looked like a professional concert place.

Which was good because it was almost two o'clock.

Concert time!

I peeked out the window of The club-house. The line to get into my backyard was down the driveway!

People in the yard were screaming.

"Secret Knock Rocks!"

"Secret Knock Rocks!"

Even Mrs. Carrick and Mrs. Roman were chanting.

Principal Not-Such-A-Joy wasn't there this time.

Her butt was having surgery.

I handed Fudgy my scarf.

"Thanks," he said, pulling out his pink, flowery one. "I'd love to trade." He handed me his scarf and then looked down at my toe. "Maybe you can use it to wrap that."

I looked down, too.

At my fence toe!

Reggie grabbed the microphone.

"Show time!" he said. He turned to me. "Sure you're okay with all of this?" he said, before heading down the ladder. "Wouldn't want to upset Miss Nabisco or anything."

I looked out at my seat.

And the thing was, I was okay.

Because when you have porcupine throat and fence toe, you might not be able to be a talented lead singer.

But you can still be a talented lead sitter.

Front row, baby!

I followed them down the ladder.

"Excuse me, excuse me," I thought to myself, as I walked to my seat. "Talented toe-scarf-wearing-lead-sitter coming through."

I took off the REEZURVD sign The Cape had put on my seat, then tapped Mrs. Roman on the shoulder. She looked surprised to see me sitting down. I pointed to my scarf toe and my not-working voice and she understood. "I'm sorry," she said with her working voice. "Is there anything I can do?" I pretended to write on the sign. She dug through her purse and handed me a pen.

Then I wrote in big letters, SMASHING GOOD ROCKS!

I held it up for everyone to see.

Pretty soon the whole place was screaming it.

"Smashing Good Rocks!"

"Smashing Good Rocks!"

I sat back down and smiled.

I knew it was going to be a good show!

Reggie came out and tapped the microphone. He pointed down to me. "This is for you, Miss Nabisco!" Then he turned to the rest of the band. "Hit it, guys!"

But it turns out I was wrong about the show.

It wasn't smashing good after all.

It was smashing great!

Heather was very tambouriney. Skipper

sounded like a professional harmonica person. And Fudgy turned out to be a very talented zebra-scarf drummer.

Even Reggie looked proud of his Little Fudger.

And he looked proud at all of us after Emma ran up and whispered something in his ear.

"Awesome," he said into the microphone. He tapped it gently. "Listen up, everyone. Great news. Secret Knock really does rock! Thanks to all of you, they've raised sixty dollars here today. Looks like you guys will be getting your dunk tank after all!"

There were cheers and hoorays for that news.

Then Reggie looked down at me.

And my fence toe.

"What are you going to do with the extra ten dollars?" he asked. "Any ideas?"

I looked over at Mrs. Roman.

And my voice decided to work for a minute.

"Buy two new scarves," it said very softly.

Mrs. Roman smiled at that news.

And I smiled, too.

Because that's what you do when your day turns out to be a SLAM DUNK!

Louise Bonnett-Rampersaud lives with her husband and two children in Sandy Spring, Maryland.

The author of several picture books, including *Never Ask a Bear* and *How Do You Sleep?*, she's working on the next adventures of **THE SECRET KNOCK CLUB**. Stay tuned for Books # 3 and 4!

Adam McHeffey is the illustrator-author of *Asiago*, a picture book about a small vampire who has a challenging day at the beach.

Also a professional musician, Adam lives in Brooklyn, New York